Also by Esther Hautzig

Riches (illustrated by Donna Diamond)

Remember Who You Are: Stories about Being Jewish

A Gift for Mama (illustrated by Donna Diamond)

The Endless Steppe: Growing Up in Siberia

A Picture of Grandmother

A Picture of
Grandmother

Esther Hautzig
Pictures by Beth Peck

Frances Foster Books
Farrar, Straus and Giroux
New York

Distributed in Canada by Douglas & McIntyre Ltd.
Printed in the United States of America
Designed by Jennifer Crilly
First edition, 2002
1 3 5 7 9 10 8 6 4 2

Library of Congress Cataloging-in-Publication Data
Hautzig, Esther Rudomin.
    A picture of grandmother / Esther Hautzig ; pictures by Beth Peck.
        p.   cm.
    Summary: A letter inviting Sara's mother and grandmother to
come from Poland to America and mentioning a mysterious
photograph arouses Sara's curiosity and leads her to discover a
family secret.
    ISBN 0-374-35920-2
    [1. Family life—Poland—Fiction.   2. Jews—Poland—Fiction.
3. Mothers and daughters—Fiction.   4. Grandmothers—Fiction.
5. Poland—Fiction.]   I. Peck, Beth, ill.   II. Title.

PZ7.H289 Pi 2002
[Fic]—dc21

                                                    2001054303

For my granddaughter
Molly Rose DeVries
with endless love

A Picture of Grandmother

one

Sara saw the fat red-white-and-blue envelope as soon as she came home from her weekly piano lesson. It was on the floor right under the slot where the mailman had dropped it. Airmail stickers were all over it. The letter was addressed to Mrs. Raya Domin, Pogulanka Street #8, Vilna, Poland. Sara did not need to look at the return address. She immediately recognized the American stamps and her uncle Benjamin's handwriting. It was just like her Mama's—big, bold, and clear. She knew it came from 960 Ocean Avenue, Brooklyn, New York, U.S.A.

Sara took off her rubber boots and her woolen leggings. She hung her coat and fur cap on the coatrack near the tiled wall stove. It had been snowing when she walked home from her piano teacher's house, and her clothes and book bag were wet. Sara put her damp hands against one of the warm tiles and dried them. Only then did she pick up the envelope from the floor. It was heavier and fatter than the usual letters. *Maybe there are lots of photographs inside*, she thought. Sara could hardly wait for Mama to come home from her pottery class.

There was always great excitement in the Domin household when a letter came from Uncle Benjamin. Mama would telephone Papa at his business. She called Grandmother Hanna. She told her younger sister, Margola, and her youngest brother, Eli. She spoke to her aunts, Rivka, Nadia, and Leah. She read the letters to practically everyone in the entire family, even grouchy old Aunt Lisa.

Of course, she read them all to Sara, too. Uncle Benjamin's letters were wonderful. Sara loved to hear about her little cousin, Stanley. He was only four years old, but he could count to fifty-five and knew the whole English alphabet. Once, Stanley wrote CAT and DOG in a letter and drew a funny small flower with red and green crayons. Sara was very interested to hear that her American aunt Dorothy loved the game of baseball. It did not matter that Sara had no idea what baseball was. If her aunt in Brooklyn liked it, it was probably as good as volleyball, which Sara often played in Vilna.

Best of all, Sara loved the photographs Uncle Benjamin sent from Brooklyn. Photographs—all photographs—were Sara's passion. She spent hours arranging them in albums or sorting them into neat piles and putting them in pretty boxes. For some she made special cardboard frames and arranged them on shelves where she kept her books.

The houses in Brooklyn did not seem much different from those in Vilna. Some were bigger and some were smaller, some were more beautiful and some were less beautiful than those on Sara's street. The synagogue on Ocean Avenue was not as grand as the Great Synagogue her family attended in Vilna. The people looked just like those she knew in Poland. But Brooklyn, New York, was in America, so it had to be wonderfully mysterious and grand. Sara wished that she could see it all for herself.

Sara carried Uncle Benjamin's letter to Papa's study and put it on the large desk where important mail was propped up by the telephone. She sat down in his big desk chair and stared at the envelope for a minute. Then she looked around at the familiar pictures of herself with Mama, of Grandmother Hanna hugging her when she was a baby, of Margola swinging her in a large canvas hammock, and at all the other elegantly framed pictures on the walls, on Mama's writing table, and on Papa's crowded desk.

Then she got up and went over to the upright piano which Papa kept in his study and sat down to practice Beethoven's "Für Elise." But she could not concentrate. She went over to Mama's little writing table and looked at pictures of Uncle Benjamin, Margola, Eli, and Mama when they were young, with Grandmother Hanna in the middle of many of the photos. Although she'd seen them all before, she carefully studied Uncle Benjamin's face because she'd never met him. He went to America long before Sara was born—even before Mama married Papa. *Mama, Mama, hurry home. I can't wait to see what Uncle Benjamin sent.* Sara had a funny habit of whispering to herself when she was alone. Once, when Mama overheard her, she said, "Well, Sara, you are talking to a very smart person!"

She went to her room to find something to read while she waited. She leafed through her favorite collection, *Fairy Tales of the Brothers Grimm*, bound in dark blue leather with gold letters and beautiful full-color pictures, which Grandmother Hanna had given her for Hanukkah. Though she loved this book, she put it back impatiently on her night table and returned to Papa's study. *I know all the stories by heart*, she whispered to herself.

Still Mama was not back.

Sara reached for the telephone and called her aunt Margola. She was barely twelve years older than Sara and was as much a friend to Sara as she was her aunt. They not only loved each other, they had fun together.

"Guess what, Margolinka?" she asked as soon as Margola picked up the phone.

"I can't guess. Too many possibilities!" Margola giggled. "But I am late for my chemistry class." Margola was a student at the university. "I promise to keep guessing until I get the right answer later today or tomorrow. I've got to run. I'm so sorry . . . Love you, Sara!"

Before Sara put down the receiver she told Margola that she loved her, too, but she wasn't sure that Margola heard her.

Sara sat quietly for a few minutes and considered what she could do next. She decided to call her best friend, Rebecca, to make the time pass more quickly.

"Guess what, Rebecca?" Sara did not wait for an answer. "There's a letter from my uncle Benjamin in America. It's huge, really big and fat. I bet it has twenty photographs of Stanley, maybe more. I can't wait to see them and Mama is not home."

Sara sat bolt upright and her eyes grew wide.

"Oh, no, Rebecca. I couldn't open it. It's addressed only to Mama." Sara paused. Her eyes grew even wider. "Yes, I know that the letter is meant for all of us. But I just can't. And I am *not* a goody-goody!"

Sara put down the receiver with a bang. Part of her wished that she did have the nerve to open the letter. After all, maybe Rebecca was right. It was meant for the whole family. Another part of her knew it would be wrong to read Mama's letter without her permission.

As she was leaving Papa's study in search of further distraction, she heard the jiggle of the front-door lock. Sara grabbed the letter and ran to the front hall. She thrust the letter into Mama's face even before she stepped into the foyer.

"Look, Mama! A letter from Uncle Benjamin!"

"How wonderful!" Mama spoke in her normally calm voice, but her hands trembled when she took the letter from Sara.

"Here, please read it right away!"

Mama took off her galoshes and her coat, but her hat remained on her head as she walked quickly to Papa's study. Using a heavy silver letter opener from Papa's desk, she carefully slit the envelope. Then, just as carefully, she took out the letter. There were no photographs inside. Instead there was a thick bundle of documents, held together with a large paper clip.

"Is everything all right, Mama?" Sara was afraid of official-looking papers. In movies and books documents always meant trouble. Mama didn't answer. Her eyes raced back and forth over the letter. Suddenly Mama raised her hands and clutched her head. The letter and all the documents scattered on the floor. "Oh, oh, oh, my goodness . . . This is absolutely amazing." Sara was dumbfounded and a little scared. Usually Mama was deliberate and careful. She did not drop things on the floor. She did not clutch her head in her hands.

"What is it, Mama? Tell me. What's the matter? Why are you holding your head? Is something wrong?"

"No, no, Sara! Nothing's wrong. It all seems like a dream!" Mama bent down to pick up the documents and her brother's letter.

"Uncle Benjamin is inviting Grandmother Hanna and me to come to the New York World's Fair this spring." Mama took off her hat and went back to Papa's desk. "He sent us the official documents so we can apply for visas." Sara wondered what visas were, but Mama was reading Uncle Benjamin's letter again and Sara did not want to interrupt her.

"Oh my goodness," Mama said again when she was finished. "Wait till I tell Grandmother Hanna. She will not believe it. I can hardly believe it myself." Mama picked up the telephone and dialed Grandmother's number.

Sara could not believe it either. *Only Mama and Grandmother would be going to the 1939 World's Fair. What about me? I also want to see America.* Sara did not whisper these words. She only thought them to herself. She left Papa's study and quietly closed the door.

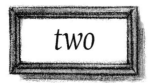

two

"Listen, Aunt Lisa, I know Benjamin never got along with Mama. But now he is older, he has a child, and he's invited her to the World's Fair. He did ask for the picture of our mother when she was young, the one where she's wearing a cameo brooch on her ruffled blouse . . ."

Mama stopped abruptly when she noticed Sara in the doorway to Papa's study. Nearly a week had passed since Uncle Benjamin's letter had come, and Mama was still discussing it on the telephone.

"Which picture of Grandmother Hanna does he want?" Sara asked quietly as she leaned over

Papa's desk toward Mama. "You didn't read that part of Uncle Benjamin's letter to me."

"Hush, Sara, can't you see that I am speaking?" Mama put her hand over the receiver.

"Yes, Aunt Lisa, I'll come next week. Yes, I'll bring Benjamin's letter. YES! He certainly did ask her to come!" Mama covered her eyes with one hand and turned away from Sara.

"Well, goodbye, Aunt Lisa. Of course I'll remember to light the candle. I am sure he will, too. Yes, yes, I will give your love to Sara."

By now Mama's cheeks were burning.

"Mama, tell me, what's so special about Uncle Benjamin's asking Grandmother to visit? Why did you have to repeat this news to Aunt Lisa so many times? It's not as if she's some wicked stepmother." Sara wrinkled her nose. "And don't bother giving me Great-aunt Lisa's love. I don't even like her. She is grouchy and she's never nice to me."

"You don't have to love Aunt Lisa. You only have to be polite." Mama took out a big linen handkerchief with a crooked hem and a white-and-yellow daisy which Sara had made her for

Hanukkah. She wiped her forehead and chin, which were wet with perspiration. Mama patted the cushion next to her on the windowsill. "Come, Sara, sit by me." They sat quietly together and watched a small flock of sparrows huddling beneath bare branches of the lilac bush that Mama and Papa had planted when Sara was born.

"Well, Mama, exactly which picture of Grandmother Hanna does Uncle Benjamin want? I don't remember any photographs of her in a ruffled blouse with a cameo brooch. Do you?"

Sara knew all the pictures in their albums and boxes. She remembered each and every photograph of all her aunts and uncles, great-aunts and great-uncles, grandparents and great-grandparents, and many, many cousins. She couldn't keep straight how some were related to each other and to her, but it didn't matter. She just liked to look at them and to hear the stories Mama and Grandmother Hanna, Margola and Uncle Eli, and Papa told her about them.

Sara knew that Great-aunt Nadia had studied philosophy in Germany. She even got a degree called Doctor of Philosophy. Sara used to wonder if a doctor of philosophy could give injections and cure sore throats.

Once, Uncle Eli told her that someday he would get a doctorate in mathematics and Margola a doctorate in chemistry. "So when you are a doctor of mathematics, will you cure me of bad grades in arithmetic?" she asked Uncle Eli. He laughed and laughed.

Sara could hardly believe that one of her great-grandmothers got married when she was fourteen, became a widow at twenty-two, raised six children all by herself, ran a business, was ramrod straight, and had hardly any gray hair when she was eighty-five. Sara never knew Mama's papa, Grandfather Hillel, but she knew that he was a lumber merchant and that Mama wished he'd had a candy factory instead. She liked to look at his photograph and imagine what he was like when Mama was a little girl. But she could not recall a picture of Grandmother Hanna as a young woman wearing a cameo brooch on a ruffled blouse.

"Maybe I didn't hear you right, Mama. Did

you say a picture of Grandmother Hanna in a ruffled blouse with a cameo brooch?"

Mama turned away from Sara. She hunched her shoulders and lowered her face until her chin was practically on her chest. Her eyes did not meet Sara's.

"What is it, Mama? Did you lose the picture? It is not in my boxes and I don't think it is in your albums. Where could it be?"

"You could say that I misplaced it. I don't think it's lost. I am quite sure it isn't." Mama straightened her shoulders and raised her head but didn't look at Sara.

"I'll help you look for it. Maybe we'll find it in the big red box in the back of your closet. Could you have put it there?" Sara flashed a bright smile at Mama.

"Thank you Sara, but it won't be necessary. I'll take care of it myself. We'll see. I just don't know . . ." Mama's voice trailed off.

Sara was used to straight answers from Mama. Yes . . . No. Mama never evaded a question.

Suddenly Mama leaned over Sara and kissed

the top of her head. Sara was surprised. Usually Mama didn't kiss her without a special reason. It was Papa who hugged and kissed her for no reason at all. But Sara knew that Mama loved her. She showed it in many other ways.

"Oh, Mama, I do hope you find the picture!" Sara kissed Mama quickly on her cheek. "But if you don't, I know what I'll do. I'll get one from Grandmother Hanna! We'll make a copy—one for you and one for Uncle Benjamin. We'll take it to the new photographer on Broad Street. I saw many wonderful photographs in his window. He changes little old pictures and makes them big and fancy . . ."

Sara's voice was trembling with excitement over her great solution to the problem.

"I'll go over to Grandmother's house tomorrow and ask her to let me look through her albums."

"Now, Sara, I want you to stop being a Miss-Do-It-All. I said I'd find the picture and I will. I don't want you to mention it to Grandmother Hanna. I haven't read that part of Benjamin's letter to her. Please don't say a single word to her about it!" Mama said, raising her voice.

Sara was alarmed and confused. Just a little while ago Mama had kissed her. Now she was angry and shouting in her ear. Tears filled Sara's eyes. She cried more than anyone in their family, sometimes for no reason at all. This time Sara had a good reason to cry.

"All right, Mama, I won't. But you don't have to shout at me. I can hear you. I only want to help!"

Sara rushed from Papa's study straight to the dining room. She ran to the sideboard and took a fistful of raisins and nuts, which Mama put out every morning in a pretty lilac-colored dish.

Mama moved from the window to the doorway. "I didn't mean to shout, and I know you have excellent hearing, Sara. And a good and loving heart." Mama swallowed hard. "I am really sorry I yelled at you."

"That's all right, Mama." Sara got mad quickly but did not stay angry for long either. Her mouth was full and she slurred her words. For once, Mama did not tell her not to talk with her mouth full, but Sara was so busy thinking how to find the lost photograph that she didn't even notice.

three

A memorial candle was glowing on the dining
room sideboard when Sara came to breakfast.
She was late. She'd spent the previous night
again going through her own photo albums with
a flashlight. Two weeks had passed since Uncle
Benjamin's letter had come, and no one had told
Sara whether the photograph of Grandmother
had been found. She was afraid to ask Mama,
she could not talk to Grandmother Hanna about
it, and Papa had been away for a few days on
business. While he was out of town and Mama
was fast asleep two nights earlier, Sara had
searched through albums and boxes in Papa's
study, too. Determined to help Mama find the

photograph, she was very curious about it herself. She was so tired that she had overslept.

Papa was finishing his breakfast just as Sara came into the dining room. He drew her to him and kissed her on both cheeks and on her forehead, too. Mama was sitting at the table. "Good morning, Sara. You'll be late for school." Sara knew that her arrival interrupted Papa's and Mama's conversation. They'd stopped talking as soon as she walked in. A sure sign that they did not want her to hear what they were saying.

"Well, Raya." Papa looked at Mama as he took a sip of tea. "It is so nice that Benjamin wrote a long letter to Mother Hanna, isn't it?" Mama nodded and gave Papa a sharp look. He did not notice. Sara did. She sat down at her place as quietly as she could, hoping not to cause another interruption in her parents' conversation. It sounded interesting. Uncle Benjamin always wrote to Mama and very seldom, practically never, to anyone else but grouchy Great-aunt Lisa. Sara never could understand why he wrote to her.

"And he also sent Mother Hanna stories about the World's Fair from *The Daily Forward*!" Papa continued. "Isn't it thoughtful of him to send clippings from a New York newspaper that she can read in Yiddish? Isn't that just wonderful? I always told you he'd come round."

Mama nodded silently.

Papa smiled and turned to Sara. "Hurry up! You'll miss your first class! It's arithmetic, isn't it? Your favorite subject!"

Sara did not smile back. Arithmetic was not her favorite subject and Papa knew it.

"Papa, what do you mean, he'd come round?"

Papa got up and stood behind Mama's chair. He put his hands on Mama's shoulders. "Oh well, I only meant that Uncle Benjamin would get around to writing a separate invitation to Grandmother Hanna to visit him in America. It's good manners, that's all. The newspaper stories made her very happy, too." He picked up his brown leather briefcase and kissed Mama.

"Have a good day in school. Remember, if arithmetic is as hard as ever, life will go on just the same." He winked at Sara, waved to Mama, and left the room.

Mama and Sara were alone at the table. "Mama, you light more Memorial Candles than anyone in our family. Who is this one for?" Sara liked the shadows that the candlelight made on the blue brocade walls.

"Someone very special," Mama answered quietly. "Eat your roll and finish your cocoa before it gets ice-cold. You'll be very late for school."

"I will, Mama, but first I want to know who the candle is for."

Mama sat across from Sara at the table and slowly sipped coffee from a large china cup. Mama was the only person Sara knew who actually liked coffee and drank it from a fancy cup. Everyone else she knew drank tea in sparkling glasses set in silver holders with rounded handles. In between sips of coffee, Mama bent forward several times to enjoy the sweet scent of a bouquet of flowers which stood in a vase in the middle of the table. Sara waited patiently for an answer to her question.

Finally Mama said, very quietly, "The candle burns in memory of someone very special, someone who has been gone for many, many years. Someone you did not know."

"Is it for your father, Grandfather Hillel?" Sara persisted.

"Grandfather's Yahrzeit, the day he died, is in August. Remember, we are always in the country?"

"Oh, yes, now I do." Sara slurped her cocoa.

"Mind your manners, Sara. You sound like Lux." Mama tried to smile. Lux was the new watchdog in their courtyard. He made a lot of noise and a big mess when he drank and ate.

"I do not sound like Lux, Mama." Sara laughed. "And I don't dribble on my fur."

Mama also tried to laugh as she came around to Sara's chair and straightened the white collar on Sara's blue school uniform. "No, you didn't dribble, that's true. But you did slurp, and you are definitely late."

Sara got up and wiped her mouth. Even though she was late, she folded her linen napkin into her initialed silver napkin ring and put it in the sideboard drawer. She dallied so that she could talk again to Mama about the Yahrzeit candle.

"I know I'm late." Sara took her school bag from under her chair. "Promise me you'll tell me who the candle is for when I come home from school. Will you?" Sara went to the hall to get her coat and cap, leggings and galoshes. It was beginning to snow again but Sara didn't mind. She loved winter.

"Sara, I won't be here when you come home from school. Grandmother Hanna and I are driving out to the old cemetery in Shnipishok. Jeremiah is taking us in his big sled with his two new horses. I am afraid to go by car in this snowy weather." Mama looked out the dining room window. Sara thought her mother's eyes glistened.

I'll be all alone at home . . . Maybe I should look in the back of Mama's closet . . . Mama looks so sad today . . . Maybe she'll be happy when I find it? All these thoughts were making a lot of noise in Sara's head. But only she could hear them.

"Afterward I will go back to Grandmother's house," Mama said as she helped Sara button her coat.

"What about your pottery class, Mama?"

"I'm not going today, Sara," Mama answered.

Sara was surprised. Mama never skipped her twice-weekly classes. "What about Papa?" she asked as she pulled her school bag over her shoulders.

"Papa has a meeting tonight at the synagogue. He will be late. Why don't you call me after you've done all your homework and we'll have supper with Grandmother, Margola, and Eli."

Sara's curiosity about the Memorial Candle abated when she heard about the visit to Grand-mother's.

"That's wonderful, Mama!" Sara grabbed her fur cap. "I'll talk to you later."

four

It was very quiet in the apartment when Sara got home from school. Snow had fallen all day. The streets of Vilna were silent and more beautiful than ever. The rooftops of houses, and the dome of the Russian Orthodox Church across the street from Sara's house, looked like pictures in one of her Russian fairy-tale collections. The fortress beyond, built in 1322 by a Lithuanian prince on top of what everyone called Castle Hill, looked as if it stood on clouds rather than in the center of the city. Sara, her cousins, and her friends often played there in good weather.

The memorial Yahrzeit candle flickered in the dining room. Sara watched it for a few minutes.

I wonder in whose memory Mama lit it, she said softly to herself. Sara decided her homework could wait. Instead she would search again for the photograph and look in the box in Mama's closet. It was the only place she hadn't yet tried.

She dragged a tall kitchen chair into her parents' bedroom. She climbed onto the chair, standing on tiptoe to reach the highest shelf. Sara had never done anything like this before and knew that she was breaking her parents' trust in her by snooping in Papa's study and now in Mama's closet. They taught by example, and in words too, the importance of respecting one another's privacy. Sara was sure that Mama never opened the diary she had begun as soon as she could write. Papa could always keep a secret when he and Sara planned a surprise for Mama or went shopping for a gift for Grandmother Hanna.

But Sara wanted so much to find the picture. She could not help herself as she pulled down the red velvet box from the uppermost shelf in Mama's closet.

She opened it carefully. Inside the box were small pieces of jewelry wrapped in dainty silk bags, a lacy, yellowed handkerchief, some velvet ribbons wound neatly in a coil, and a few envelopes written in the mysterious Russian alphabet that Sara could not read. But there were no photographs.

Sara put back all the things in perfect order and placed the box on the shelf exactly as she'd found it. The lower shelves in Mama's wardrobe held boxes of new shoes that Mama had bought for her trip to the World's Fair in New York. There were lengths of pretty fabric for the dresses to be made before she and Grandmother Hanna left for America. Mama had also bought beautiful fabric for Margola and Sara. The dressmaker who came to Sara's house to sew clothes for Mama's and Grandmother's trip would also make new outfits for her and Margola.

Sara sat down in her favorite easy chair by the dining room window and watched the snow falling softly from the sky. Her conscience bothered her—and she hadn't even found the photograph. *When all this is over, I will tell Mama that I snooped . . . I'll say I'm sorry.* Saying this to herself made Sara feel a little better. But she could not decide what to do next. She wanted to get her mind off the photograph—anyway, there were no more places at home to look for it.

I think I'll call Rebecca! She got up and went straight to Papa's study to use the telephone.

"Hello! Yes, it's me, Sara." The telephone connection was bad, which often happened when lots of snow fell in Vilna. "Who did you think it was, Shirley Temple?" Sara giggled. She was relieved to be talking to her best friend and not snooping in her parents' bedroom.

"No, I am not taking English lessons, so I really can't be Shirley Temple. Remember, silly, I wasn't invited to New York, only Mama and Grandmother were."

Sara pressed her lips together. There were many times, since the invitation had come from Uncle Benjamin, when Sara was sad that she was not going to the World's Fair. Mama and Grandmother were busy shopping, choosing gifts for Uncle Benjamin, Aunt Dorothy, and little Stanley. They had to get visas, and to learn at least a little English.

Of course, Grandmother Hanna told Sara that she would bring her back many presents, and Sara was certain that she would keep her promise. When Rebecca now asked her whether she was upset, she told her friend, "Sure, I'm disappointed! Wouldn't you be if your mother and grandmother were going to America and you had to stay in Vilna practically all alone?"

Sara sighed. "Oh, all right. I know I'm being dramatic. Mama tells me to stop behaving like some famous actress named Sarah Bernhardt, or Greta Garbo, her favorite movie star."

Sara sighed again. Then her voice brightened. "Hey, Rebecca, can you come over? Yes, right now. Yes, I know it's snowing, but you're not made of sugar, you won't melt. Even though you are sweet!" Sara needed her friend. And her good friend Rebecca came in less than fifteen minutes.

As soon as Rebecca took off the endless layers of clothes everyone wore during the endless winter months in Vilna, the girls settled down in Sara's room.

Sara snuggled in the corner of the small couch where her many dolls sat. Rebecca plopped down right next to her, putting a few of Sara's dolls in her lap and tucking her feet under her woolen skirt. Sara put a pretty plate with raisins and almonds on the lamp table by the couch so they could nibble while they talked.

"So, Greta Bernhardt, or is it Sarah Garbo, or whoever, what's bothering you so much? I know you're not being *left all alone in Vilna*! Isn't your favorite aunt, Margola, going to stay with you and your papa while your mother and Grandmother Hanna are away?"

Sara smiled sheepishly at Rebecca. "Yes, she is. And she said we can go to all the movies I like, and I can read as late as I want, every night. She said she'd let me read *War and Peace*, even on school nights. I bet she's the only person who doesn't think the book will put me to sleep."

Sara laughed. "Mama, and our librarian Dina, told me that it is too long and I should wait until I am older. But I'll show them!" Sara looked smug. "I'll even write a book report about it!" She knew she was exaggerating, but she also knew that Rebecca didn't mind.

"What is it then, Sara? You wouldn't have dragged me out of my warm house on this snowy afternoon unless you had something important to tell me."

Sara told Rebecca again about the photograph Uncle Benjamin wanted. "I've looked and looked, even though Mama said I shouldn't. I feel terrible! I only wanted to help her find it, and I can't. It's not here." Sara bit her lip.

"I think Mama lost this photograph and she won't admit it. Mama won't let me say anything about it to Grandmother Hanna. If Grandmother has it, then all our troubles will be over. But Mama won't let me ask her." Sara continued to chew her lower lip.

"Why?" Rebecca looked surprised.

"I don't know. Mama gets so upset, I don't dare talk to her about it. She is acting very strange."

"Stop it, Sara! You're making too much of it. Your mama is not strange! Besides, aren't there other members of your huge family who might have that picture?" Rebecca was being her usual no-nonsense self.

"I'm not making too much of it. And I'm not . . ." Sara stopped in midsentence and kissed Rebecca. "You are right! You've really helped me. Maybe someone else in the family does have the picture." Rebecca looked pleased and nodded.

"Mama said I can't ask Grandmother about it. But she never told me not to ask her aunts Rivka, Nadia, or Leah. Or even grouchy old Aunt Lisa."

Sara pulled Rebecca off the couch. "Let's go to Papa's study. I'll call one of Mama's aunts and see if I can go over to her house right now. Will you come with me?"

"Not in this weather, I won't. I think you're crazy, Sara. Wait until the snow stops, until it's a little warmer. There is still time before your mama and grandmother go to America."

"No, there isn't all that much time left. I am going to do it now." Sara practically dragged Rebecca to the study. "Look at some of Papa's new books while I call Great-aunt Leah. He's got a wonderful book about Ceylon, with lots of pictures of coral reefs and sea horses. He said he bought it because he and I would both like it!" Rebecca seemed interested, too.

The conversation with Great-aunt Leah was very short. "Listen to what she told me, Rebecca! 'Why do you want to go out in this awful weather?' And when I told her, she said that she was too busy to see me today."

Sara called Great-aunt Nadia next and told her right away why she wanted to come over, even in a snowstorm. "Sara, dear child, I am sorry, but I am working on a lecture about the philosopher . . ."—Sara forgot his name by the time she repeated the conversation to Rebecca— "and I must finish it by tonight. I can't be interrupted."

Sara dialed Great-aunt Rivka's number, but no one answered.

"I am very disappointed, but I'm not going to give up."

Rebecca was not surprised. She knew that her friend was very stubborn.

"I'll walk you home, Rebecca, and then I'll go to Great-aunt Lisa's. I won't even call her first. Surely she'll be home. She's too old to go out on a day like this."

"But I thought you didn't like your great-aunt Lisa." Rebecca was exasperated. "Why do you want to see her, of all people?"

"Well, I heard Mama talking to Great-aunt Lisa on the telephone about this photograph. More than once. She kept repeating 'Yes, yes, Aunt Lisa, that's the picture Benjamin wants. He wants us to bring it.' Mama described it only once. Great-aunt Lisa must know exactly which one it is."

"When you get something in your head, no one can stop you. Go if you like, but I won't go with you. Your great-aunt Lisa is not friendly."

Sara knew this was true so she didn't try to talk her friend into coming.

As they passed through the dining room, Rebecca noticed the Yahrzeit candle. "Who is it for?" she asked Sara.

"That's another mystery, Rebecca. Mama wouldn't tell me. I was late for school and I slurped my cocoa, and that annoyed Mama and then there was no time."

Dusk was approaching. Sara and Rebecca went out the door, bundled up against the snow and wind. "You can walk me as far as the Central Library for Children. Then I'll go home and you can go see your sourpuss great-aunt Lisa. I sure hope you get what you're looking for."

five

When Sara reached Great-aunt Lisa's building, she stopped and shook the snow off her galoshes. She brushed the snowflakes from her coat and cap as well. Then she walked up the marble staircase to Great-aunt Lisa's door and knocked.

Great-aunt Lisa, who was quite old and frail, peered out from behind the door.

"Oh, it's you, Sara! I didn't expect you here." She undid the door chain. "Come in."

Sara took off her galoshes and left them outside the door. Great-aunt Lisa was fussy about her house. She lived alone. Beautiful Oriental rugs covered the floor in every room, including the foyer. Sara did not want to leave any puddles on the carpets, especially when she came to ask for a favor.

"I didn't really plan to come, but my friend Rebecca and I went for a walk. Vilna is very beautiful in a snowstorm. I was close to your house, so I thought I'd stop by and say hello."

Sara knew that she was not telling the whole truth. But she *had* walked with Rebecca, she loved being out on Vilna streets in the snow, and she had a very good reason for coming to see Great-aunt Lisa.

"Well, come in, come in. This draft is giving me a chill."

Sara hurried inside. She followed Great-aunt Lisa to her big sitting room. Everyone said that Lisa was Mama's richest aunt, but she didn't offer Sara hot chocolate, or urge her to have a piece of cake, or fruit, or candy. She motioned to Sara to sit down next to her on the large sofa in the dimly lit room. They faced a long table on which Sara noticed a Yahrzeit candle flickering in the near darkness.

"What's new in your family, Sara?" Great-aunt Lisa asked. "Or is that a silly question?"

Sara didn't answer.

"I know all about your mama's trip to New York. I certainly was surprised to hear that Benjamin also invited Hanna to America."

"Well, Aunt Lisa, that's one reason I came." Sara tried to smile pleasantly. She remembered what Mama had said to her a few weeks ago. "You do not have to love Aunt Lisa. You only have to be polite."

"Do you have a picture of Grandmother Hanna when she was young, the one with the cameo brooch on a ruffled blouse? The one Uncle Benjamin wants Mama to bring to America?"

Sara took a deep breath, waiting for Great-aunt Lisa to say something.

"Remember? Mama read his letter to you. The week it came. I heard her telling you that he wanted that picture . . ."

"Why come to me?" Great-aunt Lisa's voice became gruff. "Your mama must have it."

"No, no, she doesn't. And she won't tell me if it's lost or anything. She just gets upset when I ask about it and she looks unhappy."

Sara moved into the corner of the sofa and was about to tuck her legs under her when she remembered where she was. She kept her feet neatly on the floor and her hands folded in her lap.

"I've looked for it everywhere in our house!"

"You've looked everywhere in your house, everywhere, Sara?" asked Great-aunt Lisa as she looked closely at Sara's pinched face.

"Yes, Aunt Lisa, everywhere. Mama must have lost it and this upsets her. I don't like it when she is so upset! I want to get it from you and make a copy for her so she won't be sad.

Papa will pay for it! Mama said I must not ask Grandmother about it!"

"Did she say why?" Great-aunt Lisa asked.

"No! But I bet she can't admit that she lost her own mother's picture. And I've never even seen it." Sara tried very hard to stay calm.

Great-aunt Lisa got up quickly from the sofa. She hurried to her bedroom beyond the sitting room. Sara could see her through the open door, returning with a large photo album in her hands. She immediately sat down close to Sara.

"Since you've come to ask me about the photograph, I'll show it to you." Great-aunt Lisa opened the album and put it in Sara's lap. Right in front of Sara, in the middle of the first page, all by itself, was a picture of a lovely young woman, with long hair piled high on top of her head, wearing a white blouse with a ruffled collar. A large cameo brooch was right under her chin.

"But this is not a picture of Grandmother

Hanna! This is not my mama's mama." Sara was bent over the album. She looked in confusion at Great-aunt Lisa. "I've seen pictures of Grandmother Hanna when she was young. We have them all over our house. This is someone else!"

Great-aunt Lisa's lips trembled. Her eyes were ablaze with anger. Her bony fingers gripped Sara's knee.

"This is your mama's real mama!"

Sara faced Great-aunt Lisa in disbelief.

"What do you mean, her real mama? Grandmother Hanna is her real mama!"

"Listen to me, Sara, this beautiful young woman is your mother's real mother. I ought to know. She was my sister!" Great-aunt Lisa's chin shook in anguish. "She died when Benjamin was born and your mama was three years old."

"I don't believe it. You're lying!"

Sara handed the album back to Great-aunt Lisa. She jumped off the sofa with clenched fists. Her face was contorted with fear and fury. Sara certainly forgot to be polite to Great-aunt Lisa.

"Grandmother Hanna tells me stories about Mama when she was little, about how she dug a hole to get to China through their garden and how she loved sweets, just like I do, and everything." Sara burst into tears.

"Mama loves Grandmother Hanna," Sara shouted. "They do things together. They have long talks! They help each other with things at home. *She* is Mama's real Mama!"

Great-aunt Lisa sat on the edge of the sofa and made no move to comfort Sara.

"No, Sara. Your grandmother Hanna is your mama's *stepmother*!"

"That's not true! If it was I'd know it." Sara's body shook. She stamped her foot. "Stepmothers are wicked, cruel witches. They keep their stepchildren hungry and cold. They make them work and never buy them pretty clothes. I've read all about them!"

Sara's braids came undone as she swung her head from side to side.

"Grandmother Hanna loves Mama. She always did. I have pictures of Mama when she was a little girl. She was chubby, and she wore beautiful dresses and shoes. She looks so happy in those pictures!"

Sara paced in front of Great-aunt Lisa. She knew she was being rude, but she couldn't stop herself.

"How dare you say this lady in your album is my mama's real mama. Grandmother Hanna is. A real mama is the mama who takes care of her children!"

"You know, you are named for your mama's real mama. Her name was also Sara. The name fits you well. My sister Sara also had a fiery temper." Aunt Lisa's voice shook. "Today is her Yahrzeit. It's many, many years since she died. She was only twenty-six years old then. So young, so young . . ." She turned her back to Sara and faced the candle.

Sara could not listen to Great-aunt Lisa's

words. She grabbed her clothes and her galoshes and ran out.

I'm going straight to Grandmother Hanna's! Mama said she'd be there today. They'll tell me it's not true. I know they will!

six

Sara was exhausted when she reached Grandmother Hanna's house. She carried her galoshes under her arm. Her shoes were soaked. The ribbons on her cap were untied and her coat was unbuttoned. She could hardly breathe by the time she got to Grandmother's fourth floor landing. She kicked at the door with the tip of one of her shoes.

Grandmother Hanna opened the door almost instantly.

"What is it, child? Look at you! Where have you been? Mama tried to reach you. She said you'd call us here!"

Grandmother was nearly as upset as Sara. She

took Sara's hand, just as she had done when Sara was a little girl, and led her to the kitchen. She sat her down in a well-worn chair and smoothed the hair off her wet forehead.

"Here, let me help you out of your wet things." Then she bent down to take off Sara's sopping lace-up shoes. "My goodness, even your socks are drenched."

"Grandmother, it doesn't matter. It really doesn't matter. Nothing matters to me now, nothing but one thing. Where is Mama? She said she'd be with you all afternoon, after you came back from the cemetery."

"Yes, your mama is here, but she is resting in Margola's room. She may be coming down with the flu. She had a headache and her throat was sore. I fixed hot tea, with honey and lemon, and made her take a nap."

"But Grandmother, I've got to talk to you and to her at the same time. It's an emergency. It really is. I'm not dramatizing." Sara's voice shook but she did not cry.

Suddenly Mama appeared in the kitchen doorway. Grandmother's brand-new green paisley shawl was wrapped around her shoulders—the one she bought to take to the World's Fair.

"What's this commotion, Sara? Look at you! Are you all right? You look like someone who's been in a big fight."

"Oh, Mama, I have been in a big fight. I really have."

"Where were you this afternoon? You were going to do your homework and then call me here. I called you three times! There was no answer."

"I was home for part of the afternoon, Mama, but then Rebecca came, and we went for a walk and I went over to Aunt Lisa's house . . ." Sara's voice dropped to a whisper.

"You went to Aunt Lisa's?" Mama asked incredulously. "Why?"

"Well, I wanted to see Aunt Leah, or Aunt Nadia, but they were too busy. They said so when I called them. Aunt Rivka didn't answer."

"What do you mean, they were too busy? They are always happy to see you. You must have misunderstood or had bad telephone connections."

"No, Mama, I did not misunderstand. The telephone was fine. They did not want to see me, so I went to Aunt Lisa's without calling first." Sara swallowed with difficulty. "I wanted to borrow from one of them the picture of Grandmother when she was a young woman, the one you cannot find." Sara looked down.

Mama sat down on the kitchen chair opposite Sara. Grandmother got up. She stepped behind Mama's chair and put both hands on her shoulders.

"But I told you not to ask anyone about the picture, that I'd see to it myself."

"No, Mama, you said I couldn't ask Grandmother Hanna about it. You didn't say I should not ask your aunts Leah, Nadia, Rivka, and even Lisa."

Sara looked uncertainly at Mama and Grandmother across the table. They became one person as they faced Sara.

"I was polite to Aunt Lisa. I was careful not to

make a mess on her carpets with my galoshes. I sat properly on the sofa. I didn't tuck my feet under me and I kept my hands folded in my lap."

Mama and Grandmother were silent.

"Then I told Aunt Lisa why I'd come. She brought out a big photo album from her bedroom and showed me the picture Uncle Benjamin wants. On the first page. All by itself." Sara's voice got louder. " 'This is the picture of your mama's *real* mama!' she said."

Sara shuddered as she repeated these words to Mama and Grandmother Hanna.

"I told her that she was wrong. I even called her a liar! I shouted at her and said you'd tell me that it wasn't so!"

Great sobs suddenly shook Sara's body.

"Mama, tell me! Please tell me it isn't true!"

"Aunt Lisa told you the truth. Grandmother is my mother, but Benjamin and I were not born to her. We just didn't talk about it . . . It never came up . . ." Mama seemed unable to find the right words to answer Sara.

"Why didn't you tell me? Even Margola didn't

say anything. It's not fair!" Sara looked at Mama and Grandmother in disbelief and anger.

"Sara, dear Sara! Your mama is my daughter, just as you are hers. I've taken care of her and loved her and Benjamin since they were small children. The wonderful woman to whom they were born died many years ago."

Grandmother tightened her arms around Mama's shoulders.

"Your mama was almost five and Benjamin only two years old when I met and married Grandfather Hillel. Then Eli and Margola were born to us. I think of all four of them as my children just as Grandfather Hillel did."

"Why did you keep this a secret? Tell me why!"

"Because I thought it would be better to tell you when you got older," Grandmother said softly. "You grew up with all those fairy tales about wicked stepmothers. I didn't want you to think of me as Mama's wicked stepmother." Grandmother tried to smile.

"How could you ever think that, Grandmother?" Sara did not try to smile back. "I'm not dumb. I'm not a baby!"

"There were times when I wanted to tell you." Mama looked upset and she spoke slowly. "But when I'd read you stories about Cinderella, Hansel and Gretel, Vassilisa and Snow White, I thought that Grandmother was right, that we should wait until you got older. Now I know that we were wrong. Aunt Lisa often said so."

Grandmother pulled a chair close to Sara and patted her arm. "Aunt Lisa has been angry with us for years and years because we didn't tell you about her sister. She loved her dearly." Grandmother Hanna sighed. "She resented me. But her sisters, Nadia, Rivka, and Leah, accepted me. We became good friends."

"But, Grandmother, I was sure that they were all your sisters. Whenever I looked at photographs and we talked about them, I was told that they were Mama's aunts and my great-aunts."

Mama did not interrupt Grandmother's and Sara's conversation. She sat quietly and listened. After a few minutes Grandmother continued:

"You know something? Whenever Benjamin misbehaved and I reprimanded him, he'd run to Lisa to complain. She'd give him anything he wanted!"

Sara was surprised.

"Sometimes your mama also got mad at me. But she would dig her hole to China and threaten us that she'd go there. She did not run to Aunt Lisa!"

"How come everything is all right now, Grandmother? With Uncle Benjamin I mean?"

"He's older. He has a son. Maybe he learned that you can scold a child and still love him. Maybe he and his wife, Dorothy, talked about it. Who knows, my child?" Grandmother patted Sara's back. "Benjamin was only seventeen years old when Grandfather Hillel died and he went to America."

"Now Uncle Benjamin must like you, Grandmother. After all, he invited you and Mama to the World's Fair." To herself Sara said, *He did not invite me.*

"Your mama and I got along so well! People

are different, even brothers and sisters. Both Benjamin and Mama also got along well with Eli and Margola."

"You never played favorites," Mama quickly added. "Eli got reprimanded as much as Benjamin. And who couldn't get along with our Margolinka? She was the best little girl in the world."

"Except for you, of course." Grandmother patted Sara's head. "You are the best, most wonderful, most helpful—"

"I'm not." Sara interrupted Grandmother before she could finish her sentence. "I did something really bad this afternoon, besides being rude to Aunt Lisa." Sara closed her eyes and slumped in her chair. "I took down the red box from Mama's wardrobe and looked inside. The picture was not there." Sara opened her eyes and faced Mama. "I'm sorry I snooped . . . I only wanted to help . . . I really did . . . Don't be angry . . ."

Sara, Mama, and Grandmother sat in silence for a while.

Then Grandmother spoke. "Sara, my child, everyone makes mistakes. We get angry. We forgive each other. We are a family. We love one another."

Mama nodded and turned to her daughter.

"Sara, I did keep the photograph in the red box, along with other things. You must have seen them. The photographer on Broad Street is making a special copy of the picture, just as you'd suggested. Now I will put my own copy in our photo album. I know you only wanted to help. I agree with every word Grandmother just said." Suddenly big tears ran down Mama's pale cheeks. "This has been such a difficult Yahrzeit day."

"Is it Yahrzeit today for . . ." Sara did not know what to call Mama's other mother. Mama knew whom she meant.

"Yes, it is. Grandmother went with me to her grave in Shnipishok. She stood with me and held my hand when I said my prayers. She has done it since I was a young girl." Grandmother returned to Mama and stroked her hair, as she often did Sara's.

"Will you tell me about her?" Sara asked.

"I don't remember her. I was only three when she died." Mama's face was still wet with tears. Sara handed her own handkerchief to Mama.

"Aunt Lisa said I was named for her and had her hot temper. Who can tell me more?"

"It would be very nice if you went to visit Aunt Lisa and asked her. I'm sure she would like that a lot. She must be relieved that you know the truth."

"I am so glad that there are no more secrets. That everything is in the open," Grandmother said.

"I am, too," Mama added.

I don't know how I really feel. Sara whispered so softly that only she could hear her words.

seven

Sara had mixed feelings about Great-aunt Lisa
for many weeks after their painful visit. Sometimes she was upset and angry about the way
Great-aunt Lisa had told her about the photograph Uncle Benjamin wanted. Other times she
was ashamed of calling her a liar. Sara remembered that Mama wanted her to visit Great-aunt
Lisa. But Sara prepared all kinds of excuses in
her mind in case Mama reminded her to do it.
That Mama never did made it worse.

Sara decided to talk it over with her aunt
Margola. She waited until they were together at
home one Sabbath, not during a rushed telephone conversation.

"Margolinka, sometimes I feel so bad about everything that happened. Mama said that Aunt Lisa would tell me about her sister . . ." Sara still could not bring herself to say "my other grandmother." "I know that Mama would like me to go see her. But I just can't!"

"Did Mama give you a deadline for this visit?"

"No, she didn't!" Sara was surprised at Margola's question.

"Then don't worry. Some things take a long time, other things take no time at all. You will do it when you're ready."

"Do you really think so?" Sara needed reassurance.

"Would I say it if I didn't?" Margola, like Mama, always gave straight answers.

"Thank you, Margolinka. You make me feel so much better."

Sara leaned over and rubbed noses with Margola. This was their special way of showing affection and friendship.

Margola and Sara were sitting in Sara's cozy room. It was a lazy Saturday afternoon. A mixture of snow, sleet, and rain was pounding the street outside. Sometimes Sara loved bad weather, especially when Margola, Eli, and Grandmother Hanna came for a long visit. Other family members often stopped by and stayed for supper.

When dusk fell, Papa lit a special Havdallah candle, which signified that Sabbath was over. He passed around a beautiful silver box with fragrant spices. Everyone inhaled the lovely aroma and sang a special song to wish each other a fine new week.

The following week was a good one for Sara! She got her own letter and a wonderful book from Uncle Benjamin. "I'm so glad that your mama and Grandmother Hanna are coming for a visit. I hope that someday you will also come to New York," he wrote.

Sara spent hours looking through *New York, The World's Fair City*, which had one hundred sixty photographs of skyscrapers, subways, boats in the harbor, railroad stations, the Metropolitan Museum of Art, the Empire State Building, Temple Emanu-El, the Brooklyn Bridge, the Statue of Liberty, and much more. She kept it next to her bed, together with the family photograph albums.

The week was also exciting for the whole family. Great-aunt Lisa announced that she was planning a party. It was the first party in her house that Sara could remember. That she was giving the party in honor of Mama and Grandmother's trip to America made it even more special.

Sara's doubts about visiting Great-aunt Lisa began to fade. She loved helping Mama and Grandmother Hanna with party preparations. Mama had taught her how to cut paper in fanciful patterns and glue yarn in intricate designs on cardboard. In school she'd learned how to make prints with cut-up vegetables dipped in natural dyes. Grandmother Hanna had shown her how to fold napkins to look like hats or boats or even birds. Sometimes Mama let Sara arrange flowers in small vases before she put them on their long dining room table.

"Maybe I should offer to help Aunt Lisa before her party," Sara whispered to herself more than once.

One evening, while they were embroidering napkins in the dining room, Sara asked Mama instead of talking to herself. Mama looked up from her embroidery with great surprise.

"It would be very nice of you to do that. You are very clever with your hands." Mama never complimented Sara unless she deserved praise.

"Thank you, Mama! I'll call her right away!" Sara ran to Papa's study to use the phone before she could change her mind.

"Aunt Lisa said it was a good idea!" Sara's face was flushed when she returned. "I asked whether she could forgive me for being so rude to her . . ." Sara swallowed hard. "She said that she already had . . ."

Mama nodded silently and continued to embroider. A few minutes later she got up and reached out to Sara. "You did the right thing."

Sara pressed Mama's hand to her cheek. "I love you, Mama."

A few days after her conversation with Mama, Sara began going to Great-aunt Lisa's house right after school. She spent a lot of time with her while making handsome invitations. On each one she drew a picture and cut out borders in different designs. Sara also prepared little place cards on colorful cardboard. She wrote the names of all the guests in careful block letters and made small decorations.

Great-aunt Lisa admired Sara's work.

"You are a very talented girl, Sara. Just like your mama and her mama, my sister Sara, of blessed memory, before her."

"Grandmother Hanna is talented, too!" Sara bristled. "She taught me how to sew, and how to turn collars, and to do fine needlepoint. And even how to fold napkins!"

"I know, dear, I know. I mean no offense." Great-aunt Lisa patted Sara's hair with her bony fingers. "You'll make a good defense lawyer someday."

"I don't want to be a lawyer, or a doctor." By then Sara was comfortable enough with her to disagree.

"So what do you want to become? A painter? Your mama says that you love going to museums. Or an arts and crafts teacher? You could give lessons even now. Or how about becoming a photographer?" A smile crossed her somber face.

"No, no, no! I want to become an official guide to Vilna. I know a lot about the buildings and the statues, the synagogues and the university, the gardens and the fortress in the middle of the city." Sara rattled on and on.

"I love the Museum of Folk Art. It displays beautiful clay pots and ceramics, colorful embroideries, and carved wooden sculptures made by all kinds of people. Museums are not only for paintings by famous artists! Mama says so."

Sara suddenly laughed at herself. "My friend Rebecca jokes that I should meet trains that come to Vilna, stop people when they get off, and offer them a tour of our beautiful city. Maybe even get a uniform which says WELCOME TO VILNA. And take photographs, just as you suggested."

Great-aunt Lisa laughed along with Sara. She was definitely no longer a grouch.

"Aunt Lisa, do you think this would be a good job for me?"

"It certainly would be an unusual job, my dear," she replied. "My sisters and I grew up in a small town, so coming to the big city was a special event for all of us. We could have used a good guide like you when we visited."

Once Great-aunt Lisa got started, she continued to tell stories to Sara during the many afternoons they spent together. One time Sara came to help her polish silver. She had been at the library and was carrying a huge load of books. Great-aunt Lisa was amazed at the variety of titles.

"My sister Sara also loved to read. She made up her own stories and poems, too. Some were funny and some were full of fantasy. She even illustrated what she'd written. We loved to listen to her when she read them aloud.

"When we got older our father, Reuven, made sure that we were all educated as if we were boys. That was very unusual for girls in those days. You know that my sister Nadia studied philosophy in Germany. But did you know that Leah taught history in a gymnasium? That Rivka and your grandmother Sara studied at the university in Vilna before they got married? And that I worked for many years in our father's business?"

"You see, Aunt Lisa, no one ever told me that you and your sisters were not born in the town where Grandmother Hanna was born and where she grew up. I thought that you were all her sisters. I knew that Aunt Nadia was a doctor of philosophy but I didn't know anything about Aunt Rivka and Aunt Leah, or Grandmother Sara."

Great-aunt Lisa had been about to say something when she heard Sara call her beloved sister Grandmother Sara. Instead she took a deep breath and finished polishing the silver with her great-niece.

At last, all the preparations for the party were completed. The silver was polished, the furniture was waxed, the windows were washed, the carpets were cleaned. The special day had finally come.

The big mahogany table in Great-aunt Lisa's large dining room was covered by a heavy damask tablecloth. Gleaming silver bowls were filled with exotic fruit from tropical countries. Her finest china and crystal goblets sparkled under the bright lights of the enormous chandelier over the table.

The party began when Sabbath was over. Everyone came in their finest clothes. Mama wore a blue silk dress with a full skirt and French lace around the neckline, made especially for her by a famous designer in Vilna. Papa wore his best dark gray suit, with thin white stripes, and a light gray tie. Grandmother Hanna put on her loveliest party dress, made of black moiré silk. The green paisley shawl was draped around her shoulders. Great-aunt Lisa wore a long gray dress and a silver-and-gold brocade jacket. Everyone said that she looked very pretty.

Margola wore her dark brown silk skirt and a cream-colored chiffon blouse. Even Uncle Eli, who hated to be in "party uniform," wore his fine navy blue blazer, a white shirt, and a blue tie with red stripes. Sara wore her brand-new red jumper and a white silk blouse with a round collar and full sleeves. All the distant aunts, uncles, and cousins who always came to large family gatherings were also there, dressed in their best clothes.

When they were all seated at the table, and the sacramental wine was poured by waiters hired for the evening, Great-aunt Lisa tapped her crystal goblet with a small silver spoon. Everyone stopped talking.

"I'd like to say a few words." Great-aunt Lisa

raised her voice so she could be heard even at the end of her long table. "I want to wish my dear niece Raya a safe journey to America and a safe return to us in Vilna." Everyone clapped, said "L'chaim," clicked their glasses together, and took a sip of kosher sweet wine.

"I also want to wish Hanna a happy visit and reunion with Benjamin." She looked straight into Grandmother's eyes.

Sara's eyes began to fill with tears, but she tried very hard not to start weeping as she usually did when she was happy or miserable.

"Hanna, I want to give you this little box which holds something very precious to me. I'd like you to have it now."

Great-aunt Lisa took from her pocket a small velvet box and passed it to Sara. "Here, Sara, give it to your grandmother, my child."

Sara took the box and very carefully passed it on to Grandmother, who sat one seat away, between Mama and Papa.

Grandmother looked at Great-aunt Lisa and at

the box with great surprise. She held it in her hand but made no move to open it.

"Well, open it, Hanna, open it!" Great-aunt Lisa urged her.

"Yes, open it, open it," everyone called out from around the table.

Grandmother Hanna opened the box very slowly.

"Oh, I cannot believe it! It's the cameo brooch, the one your sister wore in the picture we are taking to America."

"Yes, it is, and I want you to have it and to wear it." Great-aunt Lisa spoke very gently and softly to Grandmother Hanna.

Grandmother got up from her chair and stepped over to Great-aunt Lisa's place at the head of the table.

"Thank you, Lisa, from the bottom of my heart, both for the brooch and for your words and feelings." She bent down and hugged Great-aunt Lisa. Great-aunt Lisa reached up and hugged Grandmother Hanna.

Grandmother returned to her seat. She took a sip of water from the large crystal glass by her dinner plate.

"I will accept this gift and the honor that comes with it." Grandmother Hanna was silent for a few moments. "I shall carry the brooch with me to America as a good luck charm. I shall guard it well." Then she looked at Sara.

"And when we come back from America, I will give the brooch to Sara. When she is older she will wear your sister's beautiful pin and remember her other grandmother and namesake each time she puts it on."

Sara's eyes grew wide. "Oh, Grandmother, thank you, thank you, thank you." Papa smiled and embraced Sara. Mama gave Sara a special look and then turned her gaze to the head of the table. Sara knew exactly what Mama wanted.

"And I thank you, too, Aunt Lisa! I do, I do, I do!"

Sara got up so quickly that her chair fell backward with a loud crash. She rushed over to Great-aunt Lisa and kissed her on both cheeks.

Then she went over to Grandmother Hanna and put both arms around her neck and cried and cried and cried. No one minded Sara's crying. Everyone knew what it meant.

Afterword

My publisher suggested that I share with readers the background and origins of this story.

I was born in Vilna, an ancient and beautiful town in eastern Europe, when it was part of Poland. Its origins go back to 1322, and in my mind they are inextricably linked with learning in school that my people had lived in Vilna almost from its beginnings. Vilna, also spelled Wilno when it was part of Poland and Vilnius when it was and is now part of Lithuania, held me in its spell throughout my childhood in the 1930s.

It was an idyllic childhood, untouched by difficulties or strife, protected from the world by loving parents, teachers, a large and extended family —and enlivened by the richness of books. All of this ended when World War II erupted in Europe, and my parents, grandparents, and I were banished to Siberia in 1941 by the Soviet regime. Father was later drafted into the Russian army, and Mama, Grandmother, and I were left to fend for ourselves for the next four years.

After the war, we moved to Lodz, Poland, then on to Stockholm, Sweden, where we waited for our immigration visas to the United States. In May of 1947, I sailed alone for New York, since only I could get a visa as a student. My parents joined me a while later. Until they arrived, I lived with my mother's brother Benjamin and his family.

I was admitted to Hunter College in 1948, but left after two years when I was told that my foreign accent would prevent me from becoming an elementary school teacher in the New York State school system. Instead I turned to the field of children's literature, and worked in publishing for over forty years. I also wrote children's books and visited schools to show young people how these books were written and published.

Since 1990, I've been a weekly volunteer at the Donnell Library Center, part of the New York Public Library, and the Learning Leaders Authors Read Aloud program, through which I work in elementary school classrooms (and feel almost like a teacher) and in their Art Works program, where I lead small groups of children through the Metropolitan Museum of Art. I also volunteer in the homeless shelter at my synagogue.

In 1950 I married Walter Hautzig, a well-known pianist. We met on the boat when I was coming to America and he was returning from his first concert tour of Europe. I actually had tickets for his debut in Stockholm, but I got sick and could not attend the recital. Little did I know then that we would be married three years later. We still are, and now have two grown children.

I have written about the war years in *The Endless Steppe: Growing Up in Siberia.* Many of my other books have their origins in Vilna as I knew it before World War II, but none more than *A Picture of Grandmother* and *A Gift for Mama*, which I wrote some twenty years ago. These fictional stories grew out of very small seeds planted in me by real events in my childhood. Since they are set in a faraway time and place, I tried to be very careful in describing details: the clothes Sara wears, the home she lives in and those of her relatives, the books she reads and the movies she sees, the museums she visits and the city landmarks she loves, the seasons, the streets she walks and the shops she mentions. They all existed in Vilna in the 1930s; some still do.

Since I like to know as much as possible about the place where a story is rooted, I imagine that other readers might also. But it is always the story itself that counts the most. When I wrote *A Picture of Grandmother*, I hoped that it would resonate with readers wherever they live and whoever they are. Families are the same all over the world.